Sarah The Spider

Hilary Robinson · Illustration Jane Abbott

Belitha Press

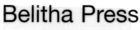

Sarah the Spider caught flies and wove webs,
Tied bows in her hair and boots on her legs,
She wore them all day, in the bath and in bed
With eight different colours, her favourite was red.

Now spiders may come in all shapes and sizes,
Some as they are and some in disguises
But Sarah was one who could dance up the walls
And sing little tunes and juggle with balls.

Her animal friends all lived on the farm
Admiring her skills, her grace and her charm
Their barn came alive when she danced on the spade
And jived in the sunshine and waltzed in the shade.

Jan Abbott

'How did you learn that?' asked Percy the Pig,
'I'm all trotters and toes whenever I jig
And catching a ball leaves me rolling about
With head over heels and tail over snout.'

'It's not very hard,' said Sarah with pride,
'I was born to perform, my repertoire's wide,
Spiders are lucky, we've eight bendy legs
In fact, if you watch, I can juggle with eggs!'

'And how do you sing?' asked Larry the Lamb
'That,' Sarah said, 'goes back to my pram
I'd shake my loud rattle and tap out the beats'
'Wow!' Larry said, 'I'll practise my bleats!'

But to Sarah the boots were her real pride and joy,
Better than any game, puzzle or toy.
She'd check them at breakfast, then later at tea
'Who would keep count, if it wasn't for me?'

At night, whilst asleep, she'd dream of the day,
When she might be the star in a leading ballet,
She felt before long her big time would come
When curtains would rise to the roll of the drum.

Waking one morning she counted her boots – 'HELP!' –
Lambs jumped at her screams, pigs squealed at her hoots;
One boot was missing, the red boot had gone!
Who could have stolen it, what had they done?

The pigs looked in tractors, the lambs behind sacks,
The hens pecked in corners, the ducks searched for tracks,
An inquiry was opened – Barney Owl was the chief –
To determine the culprit, just who was the thief?

All day Sarah cried, stretched out on her bed,
While Trixie the cat sat stroking her head,
The kind sparrows sang their bright 'chirrup' song
But Sarah was sad, her happiness gone.

Barney hid in the barn in the dark of the night
And kept a close watch as the others slept tight,
As twelve o'clock chimed, he heard squeaking whispers
And by Sarah's bed saw eyes, ears and whiskers!

Three naughty mice tiptoed round in a row,
Looked back once or twice, but they knew where to go,
They scuttled up logs next to boxes of eggs
And pulled Sarah's blue boot off one of her legs!

With a snigger and titter they ran from the barn,
Back to their hole at the end of the farm
They scurried inside – then fell flat on the floor –
For Barney had poked his head through the door!

The furious old owl was not at all pleased
Seeing Sarah the Spider so terribly teased
'If the boots aren't returned,' he squawked angrily,
'I shall eat you all up for my lunch and my tea!'

He flew away quickly, the mice were in tears,
To be eaten by owls was the worst of their fears,
As quick as a flash they knew what to do
To return both the boots, the red and the blue.

When Sarah the Spider woke up the next day
She screamed out with horror and utter dismay,
'Another boot's missing', oh what a fright!
'Barney!' she yelled, 'What happened last night?'

'Don't worry my friend,' he said with a wink,
'I've settled the problem, I very much think.'
And swooping along, flying over the floor,
He led her across to the wooden barn door.

Sarah the Spider, with lambs close behind,
Ran out of the barn, not sure what she'd find
But there, brightly polished, by the huge vats of cider,
Were the blue and red boots of Sarah the Spider.

And there we must leave her, but up to this day
Those three naughty mice have kept right away
And Sarah the Spider still dances around
With boots in the air, and boots on the ground!

For Sophie, who now thinks spiders are special HR
To my family and to Sophie, for all their support JA

First published in Great Britain in 1995 by Dragon's World Ltd

This edition published in 1997 by
🌸 Belitha Press Limited,
London House, Great Eastern Wharf
Parkgate Road, London SW11 4NQ

The catalogue record for this book is available from the British Library.

ISBN 1 85561 738 2

Printed in Spain

Editor: Kyla Barber